THE CHASE

GOD'S PURSUIT OF A YOUNG MAN

Written By

SHANE BERTHELOT

Table of Contents

CHAPTER 1

THE BARBER SHOP

It was a rainy Monday morning in Flagstaff, Arizona. I was sitting in a chair on the front porch, watching the drops fall all around me. I was patiently hoping for a break in the weather so I could walk to the shopping center at the top of the hill. While waiting, I pondered the changes about rearranging my world into a landscape I would no longer recognize.

I had waited until the last minute, as was my usual style, but I was hoping to get a haircut before my graduation night. I really didn't know if I was ready for all the upheaval that was heading my way. It was marching directly toward me. However, ready to knock me over, ready or not, I would be off to college in Baton Rouge, Louisiana in just a few short months.

My mind was heavy with thoughts about the conversations between me and my foster parents this past weekend. I was still shocked that they told me I would have to move out when I turned 18 in July. This really hurt me because I thought they cared about me. It seemed to them I was just another government check each month, and when the checks stopped, I would have to go. It was going to be a huge challenge, but somehow, I would have to make it through on my own in the months ahead.

The rain finally stopped. I peered at the dark clouds and tried hard to determine if the clouds would hold their heavy burden long enough for me to walk to the shopping center. Ten Minutes passed, and there was still no rain. I decided to try my luck and head up the hill. I was almost at the top when it started pouring. I began to run the rest of the way. I was dripping wet and out of breath when I finally made it to the barbershop. What a week I was having!

The door was open, and only the barber was inside. As I walked through the door, he turned and looked at me. The tag on his coat simply said, "Jah'camo."

"Can I help you?" he asked.

"Yes," I said.

"Do you have time to cut my hair today?"

"Certainly," he gestured toward the empty barber chair.

"Please take a seat, and I will be with you in a minute." He smiled knowingly and handed me a towel. I immediately began to dry off.

I had a seat in the enormous chair and waited for him to come over and cut my hair. By the time Jah'camo returned 20 to 30 minutes later, I was almost dry. He put the strip on my neck and draped me in the cape. Jah'camo asked, "What kind of cut do you want?"

"Just a basic haircut for graduation," I mumbled.

"You look like a man with a lot on your mind," Jah'camo observed as he expertly lifted a bit of my hair with the comb and started to cut. How could he possibly know about all the worried thoughts in my head? I sat there confounded.

When I didn't respond, Jah'camo tried a different approach, "Do you have a girlfriend?" This was a direct question that required me to answer. I told him that I just broke up with Nancy, my high school sweetheart of 4 years.

"Why?" He asked. He didn't look at me. He continued to concentrate on snipping layer after layer. I told him about college in Louisiana and that Nancy was moving to Alaska. Alaska is the kind of distance that would certainly damper any relationship. Besides, we had slowly grown apart over the past year, and it was time to move on.

At that point, I was a flowing fountain of words. I couldn't stop. I proceeded to tell Jah'camo all about my foster parents. I told him how I felt betrayed by them. I confessed that once I left Arizona, I would not be coming back. When I finished talking, Jah'camo continued to cut my hair, and for a few moments, there was silence. Then, the conversation took an unexpected twist.

"Steve, do you believe in God?" I had been in the barber chair for several minutes now, but I did not remember telling Jah'camo my name. After several seconds of silent thought, I responded, "Maybe."

Jah'camo then repeated, "Steve, do you believe in God?" Again, I hesitated.

After another moment's thought, I replied weakly, "most likely."

The Barber then said in a very firm voice, "It is a simple yes or no question. Do you believe in God?"

By then, I was getting a little frustrated. I quickly answered, "Yes!" I was feeling uncomfortable and wanted to move on quickly.

Jah'camo, however, was just getting started. His eyes showed his interest. "Have you ever prayed about the situation with your foster parents?"

"Yes, a few times," I replied dully.

"Have you ever considered this move could be God's answer to your prayers?" My only response was silence, and this apparently induced Jah'camo to tactfully switch the subject, a change for which I was grateful. No one had ever spoken to me so directly of spiritual things, at least not a stranger. Who was this guy? Finally, the haircut was over, and the barber took off the cape and thanked me for coming. I took my last twenty dollars out of my pocket and started to hand it to him for payment. Jah'camo shook his head from side to side and refused the bill. "You need this more than I do." I thanked him, carefully folding the bill and putting it back in my pocket. As I opened the door to leave the barbershop, I wondered if he somehow knew that was my last 20 dollars. The rain stopped as I left the awning shelter to start my walk home. What a strange day!

The sun dipped behind Humphreys Peak as I walked home. My foster parents were in the living room when I got home. With almost no words exchanged, we ate supper. Soon after, I got ready for bed. It was late Monday night, and I awoke from a dream, soaking wet from fear. Since the accident nine years ago when I lost both of my parents in the car crash, I've been able to remember all my dreams. I took a very hard hit to the head and was in a medically induced coma for a few days in the hospital, but eventually, I made a full recovery. I was the only survivor of the accident. Since then, my dreams have been just like reality. I still cannot decide if being able to remember all my dreams is a gift or a curse.

This dream was very strange. It started with me moving into a rental house in Flagstaff after high school graduation. I was unpacking a mound of boxes when the doorbell rang. I went to the front door, and three construction workers stood there. They asked me if I would like to pay them to remove all the rubble in the backyard where the garage had fallen. I told them to go ahead and start hauling it all off, and I would pay them when they finished.

A few hours later, one of the construction workers came to the sliding glass door at the back of the house and handed me a dirty, smashed camcorder. He told me that he found it in the rubble and insisted that it was mine. I thanked him, took the camcorder, and cleaned it up. I hooked it up to the television, which was sitting on a box against the wall in the living room. I could not believe it still worked, so I pulled up a chair and started to watch the tape that was inside. It started on the daily national news channel. They were covering a massive 9.3 earthquake on the Arizona and Nevada border. It cracked the Hoover Dam and caused great damage to several cities. The cracked dam had flooded two states: Arizona and Nevada. All the airports in the entire area were closed. McCarran International Airport in Las Vegas, Pullian Airport in Flagstaff, and Phoenix Sky Harbor had all taken big hits. Many people were dead.

The news covered all the aftershocks that occurred for weeks after the big quake, some as strong as 8.0. There were also stories about the hardship people endured after the earthquake. Children lost fathers and mothers, parents lost children, husbands lost wives, homes were destroyed, water supplies were undrinkable, and people were hurt and frightened. The coverage was very troubling, and the details of what people were going through were sad and hard to imagine.

Finally, the screen went static, and the dream ended. I awoke drenched in sweat and feeling terrified. After several minutes, I realized it was just a dream. I thanked God that it did not really happen, but I could not go back to sleep that night. Finally, the sun came up. I was never so thankful for a night to end.

The next Monday, a few days after graduation, I decided to go back to the barber shop at the shopping center on the top of the hill. When I arrived there, strangely, it was closed. I was determined to thank Jah'camo for his good advice about prayer and how God answers prayers, so I vowed to return the following day. On Tuesday morning, I hurried again through the wet grass up the hill to the barbershop. It was finally open and full of people, but I didn't see Jah'camo. When I walked through the door, the oldest of the three barbers turned and asked me, "Can I help you?"

"I'm looking for Jah'camo, the other barber who works here," I replied hopefully.

"There is no Jah'camo working here," he stated with a raised, questioning brow. I explained how I'd come last Monday and how Jah'camo had cut my hair. I told him how

I just wanted to thank Jah'camo for the advice he'd given me. The barber gave me a very strange look before explaining that he had been working at the barber shop for over 30 years. The barber shop had never been open on a Monday. Furthermore, he said there had never been a barber by the name of Jah'camo in the 30 years he'd worked here. I thanked him and left the barber shop.

Was I going crazy? Was the barber shop just another of my realistic dreams? On the walk home, I felt my hair to make sure I'd gotten it cut last week. It was definitely shorter than before. For days, I wondered about Jah'camo. I also wondered about the horrible earthquake dream I'd had the night I met Jah'camo. Was there any connection? I knew one thing for sure: It had really happened because my hair was definitely cut. I felt my newly cut strands again and was awash with relief that this strange week was finally over.

CHAPTER 2

GETTING READY FOR THE MOVE

Early in the morning, a few weeks later, I began planning my move to Louisiana. I was on the internet looking at travel sites in an attempt to determine the best time to make the move. I needed to leave a couple of weeks early since my foster parents wanted me gone by the end of July. It seemed they already had plans for my bedroom. Predictably, a new foster child would be coming on August 1st to live in my old room. I needed to figure something out quickly. I called the college in Baton Rouge about the coming two weeks early, and they transferred my call to Mrs. Ringo in the Housing Department. I explained my situation to her and asked if it would be a problem to come to Baton Rouge on August 1st instead of August 15th, the date my acceptance letter had said to move in. She told me that the Resident Assistants were the only students that came two weeks early.

"But," she said, "I have an opening for a Resident Assistant on the 11th floor of the men's dormitory if you're interested in applying for it."

It took me a second to think about it because I was afraid of heights. I really did like the sound of the new job, however. Mrs. Ringo explained that the job started on August 1st and would cover housing costs and come with a meal plan. I thought it sounded perfect for me. I asked her about the application process, and she emailed me the forms. I filled them out immediately and sent them back.

Later that day, I headed out to mow grass at a few of my neighbor's homes. For several years, I'd been doing yard work for the seniors in the community. It helped them and also provided me with a way to make a small amount of money. First, I went to Mrs. Jones's house at the bottom of the hill and cut the grass there. She was always such a nice lady. Every time I went there, she'd tell me she was praying for me. She always thanked me so sincerely that it made me feel like I had a purpose in life. I really liked going to do her yard work.

Today was different than all the other days. I explained to Mrs. Jones that I would leave for college in 6 weeks and not return afterward. I also gave her the name and phone number of my foster brother, who'd agreed to take over my work once I left town. Mrs. Jones asked me to wait momentarily and went inside the house. When she returned, she had a new Expositor's Study Bible.

She handed it to me, "Now I know why God told me to buy this Bible. You see, the writing is too small in it for me to read without my magnifying glass. But the Holy Spirt just told me to give it to you, Steve," she explained.

"Take this Bible with you to Louisiana and read it every day. In it, you will find it has all the answers to life's problems." I did not know what to say, but I thanked her and took the Bible home with me. It was a very nice Bible, and it was still shrink-wrapped. I put it unopened in my suitcase and thought it might be good to have one with me at college.

June had been a long month. I had been working hard to make enough money for the move. I checked my phone messages and got one from Mrs. Ringo at the university.

I called her back the next morning, and she told me I had the job. I thanked her and excitedly asked, "When can I start?"

"You have to be here no later than August 3rd but can come as early as July 31st." was the reply. I thanked her for the job and mentioned something about looking forward to meeting her upon my arrival at the university.

Now I had a place to stay in Louisiana! It was almost like God had helped me with that one because the timing was perfect. I still wasn't sure if it was really God or just a stroke of luck, but the coincidence was quite something! I went online to check out the ticket prices for traveling to the university. I kept hearing a small voice in my head, or perhaps it was a series of thoughts to get there as early as I possibly could. It was strange because I really wasn't in a big hurry to leave. I wanted to have time to have a few last-minute visits with my friends. I decided the "thoughts" to leave so early must have stemmed from the excitement about the move.

I checked all the bus, train, and airplane tickets online that day. The one ticket that stood out was a 6 AM flight from Phoenix to Baton Rouge on July 31st. It was 100 dollars cheaper than all the others and even cheaper than the bus fare. It wasn't a hard decision: I booked my first flight! There was a problem, however: I was afraid of heights, and flying 30,000 feet in the air would be no exception. Somehow, the excitement of the move convinced me that

I'd be ok if I sat in the middle of the plane, so I reserved a seat there.

The week before the move, the July heat was sweltering. I left the air-conditioned comfort of my home to take John, my foster brother, around to all of my customers for introductions. I really cared about them, and I wanted them to have good service for years to come. I knew John would do excellent work, which would be a great situation for everyone involved. I made sure the last house we visited was Mrs. Jones. She came to the door, and I introduced her to John. She told me she would pray for me, and she asked if I liked the Bible. I thanked her again, and after shedding a few tears, John and I left. After all, she was my favorite customer, and we had grown close over the years.

The night before, the move was stormy on several fronts, indoors and out. Samantha, my foster mom, was angry about having to get up so early to take me to the airport. We would need to leave Flagstaff at 3:00 AM to make it there in time to check in for the flight. She told me that I should have consulted her before booking a flight that early. I was very polite to her and thanked her again for saying she'd drive me to the airport.

The rain fell hard that night, and it was difficult to sleep. Lightning crashed around the house all night long. I didn't get a chance to sleep much, but I was thankful that I didn't have any dreams. When it was time to leave for the airport, my foster mom stormed into my room and told me to get ready to leave. She grumbled about the early flight all the way to the airport. I must have apologized 50 times that morning. After what seemed like an eternity, we made it to Phoenix Sky Harbor. She gave me a hug before I left to get on the airplane. "Stay in touch. Call as often as you can." I wasn't sure if Samantha had a little bit of heart after all. In any case, it was time for the next event in my life. I was excited and frightened at the same time. I hurried to board the plane and didn't look back.

CHAPTER 3

THE FLIGHT

I boarded the plane and found my seat along the middle aisle. I was one of the first to board the plane, so I got to watch everyone else come on board and sit down. Finally, the plane filled up, and a professional-looking lady in her mid-30s took the window seat next to me. She introduced herself as Julie and said she was a meteorologist for the local TV station in Phoenix. She said she was traveling to Dallas, TX, for a continuing education event on weather forecasting. I was fascinated and star-struck. I couldn't believe I was sitting beside a real TV star on the airplane!

The plane started to taxi and stopped at the main runway. The captain came on the intercom, explaining that they would take off in a few minutes and were waiting for clearance. Finally, at 6:10 AM, we took to the air. I was both excited and scared as the plane climbed to altitude. Julie could tell it was my first flight and talked to me during the climb. She was good at distracting me, so I did not have time to worry. She let me look out the window and watch the sunrise.

It was a partly cloudy day with a possibility of some rain. After talking to Julie for a couple of hours, I felt like I had made a new friend. Right before the plane landed in Dallas, Julie told me to look out our small window on the plane. There was a strange rainbow in the sky. It was flat and not curved like most rainbows, but very beautiful. It was like no rainbow I'd ever seen. I must have looked stunned because Julie immediately knew I'd never seen anything like it. She laughed at my expression and explained, "It is a fire rainbow. Fire rainbows are rare; some people go their entire lives and never see one."

She then asked me a question I'd heard recently, "Steve, do you believe in God?" I was shocked by the coincidence, so it took me a minute to answer.

I thought to myself, "Is this Jah'camo's sister?" I had already been through this once with Jah'camo, the barber in the shopping center near my foster parent's home. I knew the answer to this one. I simply replied in the affirmative. Julie smiled, saying, "Sometimes God will use the rainbow just to let you know everything is going to be alright!" I wondered why God would show me a rare fire rainbow just before the plane landed. I guess he was just saying hello!

Anyway, the plane slowly made its way to the terminal at Dallas Airport. Julie and I got off the plane and said goodbye as we went our separate ways. As she left, I almost told her to say hello to Jah'camo, but I held back the fleeting thought. I wondered at the strange coincidence.

I had to hurry to the next terminal to catch my connecting flight to Baton Rouge. I only had 45 minutes before it would depart. I ran through the terminal to the bus stop and got on the bus that went to terminal C as I was rushing to the plane. I hurried past the waiting area and caught a glimpse of the plane schedule on the wall for arriving and departing flights. Strange! Every flight to and from several cities in the West was cancelled: Phoenix, Los Vegas, and even Los Angeles. As I rushed to reach the connecting flight, I briefly wondered why. It wasn't an issue I could really ponder right now, though, since I only had a short while to make my flight. With only 20 minutes to spare, I arrived at the gate. I showed my ticket to the gate agent and hurried aboard the plane, quietly thanking God that my flight was not delayed or canceled!

The plane was much smaller than the last one. It had only 20 seats, and all of them were window seats. I was no longer afraid to sit by the window. After all, this wasn't my first flight. I had one flight under my belt and had seen my first fire rainbow, too! I sat alone as the little plane struggled to get airborne. It was not nearly as powerful as the big monster we had flown to Dallas.

It was a two-hour flight on a small plane. I put my head back on the seat and soon fell into a deep sleep. It was another dream: I had begun floating up through the clouds when suddenly, I was in a strange courtroom. This was no ordinary courtroom, however. It was white, and it seemed everyone was standing somehow in the clouds.

There was a judge sitting on a brilliant golden throne. There was a defendant and a prosecuting attorney. An assistant would call out a name, and the prosecutor would ask the judge if he could have permission to do horrible things to each of them. The defendant's attorney was a man in his mid-thirties and well-groomed but had these scars on his hands. He would occasionally ask the judge not to allow any wrongdoing. He would say, "This one is with me, and it is not allowed." The judge always agreed with the unusual attorney. Then all of a sudden, I heard my name. "Steve!" It was the assistant calling out my name. The prosecutor asked to crash the plane I was on. The other attorney said, "No! It's not his time. He's with me." Thank God the judge said, "NO!"

I awoke covered in sweat again. I was relieved the plane was still in the air and the engines were still working perfectly. We landed in Baton Rouge, and I hurried off the plane. I thought the dream was strange and that maybe some sort of underlying fear caused the dream. Perhaps next time, I will take the bus. It was late in the afternoon when I grabbed my baggage claim bags, so I got a room at a local motel. I was tired from all my new experiences, so I figured heading to school could wait until morning.

With my luggage in tow, I used what was left of my dwindling energy to rush to the curb and catch a cab. The driver took me to the local motel, only a few miles away. I wearily thanked him and had an uneventful time checking into my room. Once in the room, I ordered a pizza and soda and turned on the television while I waited for the food to arrive. I flipped through all the channels, and it seemed the president was on everyone giving a speech. In my gut, I knew something was not right. My hunger was no longer my prime concern. I stopped on a random channel and listened intently to the president's every word. He relayed information about a 9.4 earthquake and discussed how the nation would pull together after the devastation. After a few minutes, I gathered the basic details: the earthquake's epicenter was central to the Las Vegas/Flagstaff area. It had hit unexpectedly at 6:15 AM. The Hoover Dam had collapsed, and water had flooded large areas in two states. Airports in the affected areas on the West Coast were closed for the rest of the week, and the president encouraged all residents to remain at home until further notice. He said the government would help all those who needed help.

I immediately tried to call my old house to see all the people I knew there, but the phone lines were down. I tried to call Mrs. Jones, but the phones were not working again. The television had said that Flagstaff and Phoenix were two of the hardest his areas, and there were many fatalities. I started to cry and began to pray for my friends and family there. I also thanked God for allowing me to escape just in time. I was shocked that my dream had come true. I wondered why

I had such a listening problem because God had warned me many times. I took out my computer and did several searches on the internet. I just had to search for Julie. I looked at all the local television in the Phoenix area, and, just like with the Barber, no one worked at any of the television stations named Julie. I started to think that she must have been an angel sent to make sure I made it to Louisiana safely.

After my last dream, it seemed the devil was trying to get permission to crash my plane. He was upset that I got off the ground five minutes before the earthquake hit. I decided at that point to take God more seriously. I took out my new Bible, which Mrs. Jones had given me. I opened it for the first time and spent the rest of the day reading it like a new book I could not put down. I read it for several hours before falling asleep. Thank God I did not have any more dreams that night.

CHAPTER 4

THE ARRIVAL AT THE UNIVERSITY

I got up early the next morning and checked out of the hotel. After grabbing a cup of coffee and Danish in the lobby, I caught a cab and headed straight to the university. What a

Difference from the West! The water was so plentiful here that the plants were larger and greener, especially the trees.

I got out of the cab and followed the signs on the path to the Housing department, but the main area of the department was empty. I searched upstairs and found Mrs. Ringo's office, but she hadn't arrived for work yet. I sat on the floor

Outside her office door and waited. Finally, I saw a large African American lady coming up the stairs using a cane to aid her. She looked to be about 60 years old. She came to the Office door where I was waiting and peered down at me, "Can I help you, young man?" I quickly got up and said,

"I'm Steve, and you must be Mrs. Ringo."

"Yes," she replied warmly.

"Great to meet you, Steve. Come on inside. I have paperwork for you to fill out before we head to the dormitory."

After completing the paperwork, Mrs. Ringo took me to the dorm in her car, a very tall rectangular concrete building. The rooms were situated so that the doors faced the outside of the building on each level. 3-foot high railings protected the walkways. I noticed the elevator was out of order. Mrs. Ringo gave me my keys and explained that my room number was 1101 on the 11th floor. My key would open any door in the building. She told me to go and get myself unpacked. Orientation was in just a few days, and all the other Resident Assistants would soon arrive. I should be prepared to work by then. I was excited and headed up the stairs alone. At first, it was easy, but by the time I got to the top with my suitcases, I was out of breath and a little shaky. I paused at the top of the stairs and looked out the window to a gorgeous view of the city. Unfortunately, I could only look out for a brief moment because I was suddenly overcome with fear. I quickly found my room and went inside. I had to sit on the bed for a minute and get myself back together, as my fear of heights had shaken me. After several minutes, I unpacked my suitcases, and I didn't leave the room again that day.

There was a big storm that night with thunder and heavy rain. After a whole night of tossing and turning, I eventually got to sleep and had another dream. I was sitting in room 1102 with my suitemate, counting hundred-dollar bills. He was a large, heavy-set Mexican American man wearing a suit and tie. He was talking on the telephone about the money someone owed us. He and I were in some kind of business together, making a lot of money. All of a sudden, there was a loud knock on the door. Then a voice boomed out, "Open the door now! This is the Police!"

My suitemate hung up the phone and ran into the bathroom that connected our two rooms. They must have had a master key because the door was open before I could even react. I was pulled off the bed and handcuffed. They asked me if anybody else was in the room, and I directed them to the bathroom. The police went into the bathroom and then room 1101 but found no one. My suitemate had apparently gotten away, leaving me holding all the evidence.

As the police led me out, I awoke! I sat on the bed for a while, shaking with fear and sweat. I had not yet met my suitemate and was already dreaming about him. I returned to sleep after an hour or so and didn't wake up again till daylight.

As I climbed out of bed, I prepared myself for the coming day. At about 9 AM, I headed out in the bright morning sun to the Campus financial building to see about my student loan. It took almost 15 minutes to walk to my destination, only to find a long line with only a single man working behind the glass. After an hour-long wait, I finally got to the window, and the gentleman proceeded to hand me a stack of twenty and hundred-dollar bills. I only got half of what I borrowed, with the other half held for the university fees. I was happy to have such a large amount of money in my pocket. I went to the bookstore on campus next, only to find it was closed for lunch hour.

As I walked away from the bookstore, it started to rain hard. I ran back and took shelter under the overhang at the bookstore, but I only got a little wet. After what seemed like an eternity of watching the drops fall from the sky, the bookstore reopened. I went inside to find only one elderly lady working whose name tag said "Carol." I located the campus catalog that showed which classes I needed to take for each degree, and I headed to the register to check out.

"That will be five dollars," Carol said tiredly. I gave her a $5 bill and waited for her to put my catalog in a plastic bag, since it was still raining. She put the book in the plastic bag and gave me $95. I was initially shocked, but she said without explanation, "That is the correct change. You have a nice day!" I managed a garbled "thanks" and left the building very quickly.

I felt guilty as I walked back to the dorm room, but I knew I could always use the extra money. It started raining even harder when I was halfway back to the dorm. Lightning began to strike all around the campus. I ran as fast as I could back to the dorm. When I got back and headed up the stairs, I noticed a few students on the lower floors. As I arrived on the 11th floor, I was still dripping wet. I did not look out of the window this time. I wanted to avoid exacerbating my fear of heights.

When I arrived in my room, I put the $95 on the desk as if I would return it. I did this in case Carol realized her mistake and came for the money. The sun had set, and I slept that night without any interruptions. The following day, I awoke early to find the money still on the desk. As I put it away, I still felt guilty but found that the guilt had faded some. I quickly forgot about the money and headed to the cafeteria for breakfast. It was only a short walk, but it started raining again when I was halfway there. I ran as fast as I could, but I was soaking wet by the time I reached the cafeteria. I went through the line and got the few things I wanted. When I got to the register, I was greeted by the same elderly lady I'd seen at the bookstore. It was Carol. I asked her if she worked at both places. She shook her head. She said her register came up $95 short, and they demoted her to the cafeteria for a slower pace. She said if it happened again, she would be fired! I was still dripping wet, so I sat down at the far end of the cafeteria. The guilty feeling had returned in full force. I ate as quickly as possible and returned to the dorm, ignoring the rain. As I went up the stairs, I wondered if I should buy an umbrella since it seemed like God would cause it to rain every time I left the shelter of the building.

The next morning, more of the residents arrived. My floor was starting to fill up. That afternoon, we had our first resident assistant meeting downstairs. I got to meet all the RA's and the dorm director, Robert, who instructed me to go around my floor and meet all the residents. I headed back to the 11th floor and met all the residents. I headed back to the 11th floor on the elevator for the first time. It was a bumpy, noisy ride. The elevator made several loud noises and jerked up and down several times. I got a notebook from my dorm room and headed around the floor to meet the residents.

All the residents were so different from one another. There were two skydivers in room 1105. Room 1115 had a surfer, but I didn't know where he would surf around Baton Rouge. The last room on the right was 1120, which was where I found two guys dressed like women. What else would I find as I returned to my room and knocked on room 1102? The occupant opened the door, and I noticed the room was filled with a very strange-smelling smoke.

I introduced myself, and he grinned widely, "I'm Howie, the president of the campus fraternity." I was surprised, as he was very heavy-set and greatly resembled the man in my dream. I tried to respond naturally, saying it was good to meet him, as I wrote his name on the notebook and quickly headed back to my room. I was glad to get away and into the fresh air. I could hardly breathe in there!

CHAPTER 5

CLASSES BEGIN

I was so excited that I awoke in daylight. It was Monday morning, the first day of classes! I tried opening the bathroom door to shower, only to find Howie was already there. When Howie finished, I had to rush to prepare and not be late for class. I was starting to wonder about Howie. If this was his daily routine, it could be a real problem as school progressed. Still, he was always friendly, even if he had nothing else going for him.

I walked to class and was surprised there was no rain this time. Maybe it was all in my head that God was mad at me!

I went to all my classes that morning only to find Howie was in my chemistry class, and, of course, he came and sat at the desk right behind me. Life at the university was going to be very interesting and challenging. I was great at math and English, but chemistry was something else. I suspected Howie was sitting behind me so that he could cheat on the test. Did he have a surprise coming if that was his plan?

It was lunchtime, and I headed to the cafeteria full speed ahead! I wasn't surprised to find Mrs. Carol working on the register again. I no longer felt guilty about what happened. I gave her my school ID this time, and she swiped it! I had $800 left on it for food. The school gave me money for food with my RA job in the dorms. However, I quickly figured out I would run out mid-semester. Either I ate too much, the food was overpriced, or, most likely, both! In any case, it was good to see that Carol was doing fine. I now understand why management had moved her to the cafeteria. Most of the students had ID cards with credits, so very little money changed hands. I slumped down at the first open table and started eating my pizza when two guys I recognized sat beside me. It was the skydivers from the

11th floor, Jeff and Mike. They asked me how I was enjoying school, and, of course, I told them that it was great so far. We started talking about skydiving, and they told me they had been doing it for over a year. I asked them why they did it, and they gave me a strange answer. They said that it made them realize how short life was and that it was not what I expected at all! Then they invited me to go skydiving with them that weekend. I did not want to tell them about my fear of heights, so I told them I'd give it some thought. I was finished and headed back to class again. As I walked, I thought about how good it was to have new friends, but I wondered about my choices. Howie was a very strange character, to say the least. Mike and Jeff were two nuts, for sure! Classes for the day were finally over, and I returned to my room. Just when I started to relax, a knock came on the bathroom door.

I knew it had to be Howie, "Oh boy, this guy just won't go away," I thought. I was friendly as I opened the door, and he entered the room and sat down. I was friendly as I opened the door, and he entered the room and sat down. I asked him to please not smoke in my room.

He laughed and said, "I only smoke that stuff the day before the semester starts to celebrate new beginnings." I was glad to hear it. Howie had asked me if I wanted to go to a car auction with him on Saturday afternoon. I agreed.

Later that night, I did my final round, walking the floor. To my surprise, all was peaceful, and no residents were out. I went back to my room and turned in for the night. Unfortunately, I had another dream. I was on a huge cruise ship sailing to the Hawaiian Islands this time. There was a very attractive young lady who really stood out. She was only about 4.5 feet tall, very slender, and appeared in her early twenties. She was speaking to a young man. Somehow, I knew he was not her husband. I found them sitting across from me at the dinner table each night on the cruise because there was assigned seating. She was easy to recognize because of her bright red hair.

One night, I found her alone on the deck and got to speak to her very briefly. She asked for my help. She explained that she was addicted to drugs and needed to get away from everything, especially the people who were currently her circle of friends. I quickly ended the conversation and headed back to my room. On the last day of the cruise, right before departure, I saw the same lady again. This time, she was much older and alone. She now walked with a cane. The wind was blowing hard, and papers were blowing around the deck everywhere.

As I leaned over to pick one up, she recognized me and, surprisedly, came over to talk to me. "Where were you?" She asked. "Why did you not come to help me?"

Turning before I could answer, she walked away slowly with her cane. I soon lost sight of her as she disappeared into the stairway. I felt very guilty as I awoke.

I did not fully understand the dream or what it was trying to tell me, but I figured it might be important, so I played it over and over to remember the details clearly.

When Saturday came, Mike and Jeff knocked on my door early to ask if I was going skydiving with them, I apologized and said I had made other plans. I explained that I would go to the auction with Howie that afternoon. They quickly told me to steer clear of Howie, for he was trouble.

"Thanks for the advice," I responded, "But I need a car, and Howie will have to do since he's my ride to the auction." They both looked worried but told me to have a good weekend. A few hours later, a very loud and forceful knock came on the bathroom door. I opened it to find Howie with the usual grin on his face. He wore colorful Hawaiian shorts and a bright green and yellow T-shirt! Howie was very different from most Latinos because he didn't speak a single word of Spanish.

When I got to the parking lot, I discovered Howie's car was a twenty-year-old moped! He asked me to drive, so I agreed. We both hopped on the moped and headed to the auction. Altogether, we both must have weighed 400 pounds! I thought the tires were going to blow at any time. The route took us on a very busy freeway with cars speeding around us at fifty to sixty miles per hour. It didn't seem to bother Howie. I guess he was used to it, but I was terrified! Just as we reached the fairgrounds and I let out a sigh of relief, I heard a loud siren behind me. I looked in the rearview mirror to see blue lights! It was a police officer wanting to stop me. I should have known better than to go anywhere with Howie. The officer explained that I was going too slowly. He said I shouldn't drive a moped on this street because it was dangerous. "Great, I'm going to get my first ticket for going too slowly," I thought. The officer told me not to worry. He said just to be sure to pay $95 for the ticket before the date due, and all would be well. I thanked the officer and turned into the auction with Howie

on the back, laughing at me.

"That's a first! I've never got a ticket for going too

slow," he mocked me as we got off the moped. I didn't

respond because I was in deep thought. The ticket price was

the same amount I took from Carol, the nice elderly lady in

the college bookstore.

An hour into the auction, a huge rainstorm blew in

from nowhere. They had just started to auction off the car I

wanted: a bright green Ford Pinto that was 20 years old. It

did come with new tires. I bid first at $300, but to my

surprise, Howie bid $400. I looked at him and told him to

stop, but he was laughing hard as the rain started to come

down. Next, I bid five hundred dollars. Luckily, Howie did

not bid this time. Going once, going twice," the auctioneer

cried. "Sold for $500 to the young man in the rain!"

They declared the auction over because of the storm.

I was soaking wet again, but we put Howie's moped in the

trunk and drove the car home in the storm. "What a weird rainstorm from nowhere," Howie said. "Get used to it. God is mad at me, and it rains on me every day," I explained. "Wow!" Howie exclaimed! "No big deal. God is mad at me, too! He does not like my daily activities, but the rain is something new." It was good to get back to the dorm. I relaxed and prepared for upcoming class sessions for the remainder of the weekend.

CHAPTER 6

SKYDIVING

It was Wednesday morning, and I hurried to chemistry class because we would get our first test grades back. The elderly teacher walked around the room, passing out the exams. She handed me my paper, which had an 83% B- marked red in the top right-hand corner. Next, I saw her stop at Howie's desk. "Congratulations, Howie! Class, Howie got a perfect 100 %! It's only the third one in my thirty years of teaching. Subsequently, there will be no curve on this test. Congratulations again, Howie, on the great work."

I was shocked because Howie had not been to class since the very first day of the semester. He only showed up to take the test. He definitely did not cheat on me or anyone else. How did he do it? Howie was certainly not the sharpest tool in the shed, so to speak. I would just have to study harder and try to get my grade up since it didn't look like there would be any curve with Howie in the class. Later that day, I returned to the dorm and ran into Jeff and Mike, who asked me to skydive with them on Saturday.

They claimed to know everybody, insisting it would cost me nothing. How could I say no to a free skydive? I immediately said yes. I would overcome my fear of heights once and for all. That afternoon, I planned to take care of a few errands. First, I would pay for the speeding ticket I already had in the envelope. I mailed the $95 money order to the judge. I dropped the envelope in the mailbox in the dorm's lobby and headed straight for the cafeteria. As I went through the line, I noticed the girl in front of me looked strangely like the one in the dream. She was very attractive and had beautiful red hair. I had to at least speak to her and try to strike up a conversation. I did not want a girlfriend, but maybe she needed help. I said hello and introduced myself as we went through the line. She said her name was Sally. When we got to Carol, the cashier, Sally had forgotten her ID, so I stepped up and paid for her meal, too! My "dream girl" thanked me and asked me to sit with her. We had a good conversation, and she invited me to play tennis with her next week. As I left, she gave me her phone number and thanked me again.

When I got back to the dorm that night, there was a loud knock on the bathroom door. It was Howie again, wanting a ride to the store to get some supplies and a movie. He began Telling me how someone stole his moped and the cops could not find it. I was nice about the whole situation and brought him to the store in my old car, even though I did not feel like it.

It was hard to tell Howie no! He had a way about him that was very persuasive. On the way back, I asked him how he did so well in chemistry. He said he would tell me one day, but I was not ready yet. I wondered what he meant but didn't ask. We arrived back at the dorm, and each of us went to our rooms.

There was a storm that night. As I lay on the bed, I read the Bible for a while. The thought of going skydiving that weekend was terrifying to me. I did not believe I was right with God yet, and maybe I would die if the parachute failed to open. Because of my pride, though, I couldn't back down now. I was going to jump, but I was really hoping and praying that the weather would cancel the Saturday adventure.

As I fell asleep that night, I began to dream that I was standing before a great white throne. The man sitting there was dressed in white with scars on his hands and feet. I was standing in line with many other people. I slowly came to the front of the line, knowing I'd be judged. It was terrifying because no one was found innocent. The man in the white cried as he sentenced everybody in the line, one at a time, to eternity in a lake of fire. An enormous angel would escort each person after they were sentenced. When it was my turn,

I was scared and physically shaking. My life flashed before me, and I was so ashamed! I realized that the man on the throne was Jesus, and I had wasted my life. Just when he started to me, I awoke in a puddle of sweat. It took me a few hours to go back to sleep, and the storm roared in the dark of night.

It was finally Saturday morning, and I awoke early to check the weather for the day. It would be sunny and 80 degrees, with no clouds in the sky. Before I knew it, there was a loud knock on the door. Jeff and Mike were both excited and ready for the skydiving adventure. Before we left the dorm,

They wanted to pray that the day would be safe and that God would bless all of us. We then left for the drop zone, which was about a 30-minute drive. It seemed like the longest drive of my life. I asked God to help me all the way. As we pulled into the parking lot, they asked me if I would like to accept Jesus as my savior. With the dream about the Great White Throne, the man crying as he sentenced the people in line, and the lake of fire fresh in my mind, I eagerly responded with a "yes." They prayed with me there, and I asked Jesus to forgive my sins and to become my savior and Lord.

We went inside the hangar at the airport, where Jeff and Mike introduced me to all the skydivers. I was shocked to find a doctor, lawyer, and pharmacist there. It seemed everyone was skydiving from all walks of life. After 5 hours of classes and practice, it was time to jump. I would do my first jump solo on the static line.

The plane quickly took off. I saw that they took out all the aircraft seats except for the pilot's seat. Jeff put me next to the door, and then he opened it. He told me to look straight down and use the landing gear as a reference site to tell the pilot left or right, 5 degrees or 10 degrees.

Finally, when I thought I had the plane in the correct place, Jeff verified it and told me to climb out on the wing. Without looking down and terrified of what I had done, but knowing I was right with God now, I climbed onto the wing, and off I went! The parachute opened in just a few seconds, but I didn't do anything correctly. Then I heard a voice come on in the helmet telling me not to worry. He said that I would do better next time. He told me to turn left. It was as if I could hear the voice of God inside my helmet! The voices were only Jeff and Mike having a good time. I pulled the toggle and turned left. The voice told me all the way down to a hard landing.

I fell forward and rolled onto the ground as I was taught. I had survived my first skydive without any major injuries! I was so excited! I felt like Superman! After 30 minutes, the adrenaline wore off, and I was back to normal.

Now, it was almost dark, and the last skydivers of the day landed. When all the skydivers started breaking out the beer, Jeff and Mike said it was time to go. We all left and headed back to the dorms. I thanked them both for everything, and they invited me to church on Sunday. "Yes! I'd be glad to go," I replied eagerly.

CHAPTER 7

THE ELEVATOR

It was early Wednesday morning, and I was again walking to chemistry class. It was a dark, dreary day with looming black clouds overhead. To my surprise, I saw Howie ahead of me. He was heading toward the chemistry building. I hurried ahead to catch up with him. When I caught up with him, I was out of breath, "Are you ready for the test?"

He laughed and then replied smugly, "I'm always ready." "How do you do it? You haven't even been in class," I asked. Howie just laughed again, "Don't worry. The test will be easy." As I took my seat, I noticed that everybody, except Howie, looked stressed, and nobody said much. Then, the teacher entered the room and started passing out the test. The test was hard as expected, but I studied carefully and knew more answers this time. Of course, Howie was the first to finish and rushed to turn in the test paper before leaving the room. I finally finished and was excited to turn in the test and go.

It was lunchtime, so I headed straight to the cafeteria. It was good to see Carol again at the register. As I paid her for the meal, she told me my meal plan was starting to run low and that I should look into purchasing some more credits before it ran out! I was shocked that I only had $275 left on the meal card. I definitely needed to cut back on meals or buy some more credits. I was happy to see Jeff and Mike again at the far end of the cafeteria. I hurried over to their table and joined them in conversation as we ate. We talked about the Bible, and they asked me if I had anything I needed them to pray for. "Yes," I responded quickly, "I sure could use God's help on the chemistry test I just took." To my surprise, they stopped eating, hopped from the table, then came over to my seat, kneeled, and started praying with me. After the prayer, I was thankful for the help with chemistry, but I was a little embarrassed that they prayed so openly in front of everybody. Maybe God would help me with my chemistry grade, so it was worth it! After lunch, we all headed back to the dorm because my classes were over for the day, and I had Resident Assistant duty that night.

I was walking the floors later that night, checking the dorms one last time before bed. The moon was full, and the wind blew hard without a cloud in the sky. I walked every floor around the building. There was almost no one out on the balcony this time of night, and it was quiet and peaceful. Finally, I made it down to the first floor. To my surprise, Jeff and Mike were hanging out by the elevator, passing out fliers for the upcoming concert at the church! They were excited to see me. They gave me a flier and began asking me about my day, when we all saw two large, muscular students appear with a young girl in their arms. They were holding her up, for she had clearly passed out!

They hurried to the elevator with the girl, almost dragging her along. I asked them to stop for a second. They did.

"What do you want, RA," one of them asked.

"You can't bring that girl up the elevator. Visitation is over."

"It's only 11:55 PM. Visitation is over at midnight," replied the same guy. They both laughed as the doors to the elevator closed.

"Aren't you going to stop them," questioned Jeff.

"Help me see where they went," was my reply. Using the stairs, we all headed to the parking lot, Hoping to see from outside the building which room they went into. We were too late, however. I had never seen them before, so I had no other options. Shrugging, I returned to my dorm and turned in for the night. I tossed and turned the entire night. I worried that I had let the girl in the elevator down. It seemed this RA position was a lot more than I bargained for.

Friday morning came, and I was off again for chemistry class. I hurried along the path, excited to see if God answered the prayer that Jeff and Mike sent up in the cafeteria. I arrived in class, and to my surprise, Howie was already there. I thought to myself, I got you this time, Howie. God is surely on my side. Class, the teacher explained as she passed out the test, "There was no perfect score this time. However, Howie made another A, so there will be no curve."

I got my test back, and it read 86%B. Not bad, but I was very disappointed because I knew good Christians sent up the prayer, and God had to answer it. Oh well, I guess God was busy or something. I did not understand but knew better than to hold it against him. Maybe next time, I will pray before the exam!

After class, I returned to the dorm since it was Friday evening, and I just wanted to relax and enjoy the week's end. At around 9 PM, there was a loud knock on the door.

"Steve, are you there? I need your help," a voice cried out. I opened the door to discover it was Howie.

"What do you want," I asked. "I need a ride to the store to pick up some soda and movies for the weekend," was the response.

"I have a girlfriend visiting this weekend. You won't write me up; will you?"

"Howie, I'm not on duty this weekend, but if I hear you after hours, I will have to write you up."

"Ok, could you please take me to the store? The police still have not found my moped." He gave me a pleading look, so I reluctantly gave in.

"Ok, Howie." There went my relaxing weekend. On the way back from the store and a few blocks from the dorm, the car started to sputter and then stopped.

"What's wrong with the car," asked Howie."

"I'm not sure, but can you help me push it off the road?"

"Of course," he replied, and we pushed the car into an abandoned parking lot. Then, we walked back to the dorm. Howie thanked me for the ride and went back into his room. I decided to deal with the car later, so I returned to my room for some much-needed rest.

The entire time, I kept thinking that if only I hadn't given Howie a ride to the store, then maybe the car would still be fine. It was so hard to tell him no, though!

The following day, I had the car towed to a local garage. It ended up costing $340 for the repairs! I was furious and blamed Howie for creating yet another unnecessary cost, but I supposed that I was supposed to be good to him as a Christian. Maybe God would turn it for good and help me more on the next chemistry test.

It was Saturday morning, and I woke up late. I called Sally to see if she wanted to play tennis that weekend. I dialed her number, and the phone rang several times before an answering machine picked up.

"It's Sally," the machine began, "Maybe I'm here, maybe I'm not. Maybe I'm in the shower, getting really hot! Leave a message, and I might call you back!!!...beep!"

"Sally, it's Steve. I was just wondering if you wanted to play tennis this weekend?" Well, I guessed Sally was busy. It's good that I was only interested in helping her because the dream said to. I just left a message and wanted to see if she called me back. If not, I would just spend the weekend studying chemistry and maybe writing up Howie!

CHAPTER 8

THE TENNIS MATCH

It wasn't until Thursday that I finally heard from Sally. I woke up to the phone ringing at 6:30 AM. To my surprise, it was Sally asked if I was ready to play tennis that weekend. "I'd love to," I replied eagerly.

We made plans to meet at the tennis courts at 11 AM on Saturday. This was exciting for me because maybe I would finally understand why I'd had the dream about her. I knew she was in trouble from the dream, but I did not know why. I also knew that I needed to buy a tennis racket and find some information on tennis before Saturday since I'd never played before. How hard could it be?

After a good morning in class, I headed to the cafeteria for lunch. After another trip through the line and selecting my meal, I ate roast beef and mashed potatoes with a piece of apple pie. To my surprise, Carol said that it would be $5.

Why? I asked, "I have a lunch plan." She responded that you had a lunch plan, but it's all gone.

"That will be $5, please." I gave Carol a ten-dollar bil; inn return, she gave me $50 in change. This time, I decided against taking advantage of Mrs. Carol.

"Mrs. Carol, I gave you $10.00, and you gave me too much money back."

"I'm sorry," she said and returned the money, giving me the correct change. $50 would have paid for my tennis racket and book, but my umbrella was broken, and I didn't want to test God again.

After getting past the register and Carol, I looked for a seat and spotted Howie sitting by himself at the window. I rushed over and went to sit across from him at the table, deciding to say nothing about the $340.00 car repair bill.

I asked, "How are you, Howie?"

"I finally got my moped back."

"Was it damaged? Did they catch the man that stole it?"

"It was a woman," he laughed, "and she did not get caught." "How do you know it was a woman?"

"Because they painted it pink. I can't go anywhere on it until I repaint it."

"Oh. Just let me know if you need a ride somewhere."

"By the way, Steve. In a few weeks, I could use your help filling out my study guide for the chemistry test."

"I'll be happy to help you, Howie!" I couldn't believe I said this after what it cost me the last time I helped him.

After lunch, I returned to the dorm room to rest for a few hours before shopping for the tennis racket. During my afternoon nap, I had another dream.

I was at a large pond in the middle of nowhere, fishing all by myself and having the best time. It was very peaceful and quiet, but then, all of a sudden, the water splashed, and something tugged my line. The line went tight, and the rod and reel started to spin. I was in the fight of my life!

I fought with the fish for at least 15 minutes. It took almost all of the line, but I finally got the fish to shore. It was a huge bass that weighed at least 18 pounds. I was so excited that I woke up.

I quickly decided to go fishing the following weekend since I would play tennis with Sally.

It was now late Thursday afternoon, and I headed to the local shopping mall. After sifting through a large crowd, I finally found the store with everything I needed. I wished I had the extra $50 that Carol had tried to give me, but I was glad I'd done the right thing.

After several minutes of looking, I found a cheap tennis racket and fishing pole. I would have to skip the book on tennis and try to figure it out on Saturday. I simply had to save the extra money because I knew I would need it for the cafeteria for the rest of the year. Maybe I would catch some fish and cook them in my dorm room, which would save money, too! After shopping, I headed back to the dorm for a good night's rest.

Finally, it was Saturday morning! I had been looking forward to playing tennis with Sally. I got up early and went on the internet to read about playing tennis. I was glad I had because I discovered several rules to the game that I needed to know before showing up there. I didn't want Sally to know I never played tennis before.

I arrived a few minutes early at the tennis court, only to discover Sally was already there. She was beautiful as always, wearing white shorts and a white blouse. Her bright red hair glowed in the morning sunlight. After a few minutes of small talk, we got down to business. The first set didn't go well for me.

I lost 6 to 0, or love, as they say in tennis. She felt sorry for me because I started winning and won the second set 6 to 4. We played one more set, and Sally beat me 6 to 1. After tennis, Sally and I sat on a bench and talked for a while. Then she asked me what I was doing that night. "I don't have any plans," I replied a little nervously.

"Well, I'm going out," she continued. "I have some fresh weed we can do."

Shocked, I explained that I was a Christian and simply could not do anything like that! After a few more minutes of small talk, she thanked me for the tennis match and said maybe we could do it again.

It was late afternoon, and I went back to the dorm to rest and get cleaned up. It had been a very interesting morning with Sally. I was happy since I finally knew why she needed help. I didn't know what to do for her but to pray, so when I got back to the room, I prayed for Sally before cleaning up.

On Sunday morning, I awoke at 5 AM. I headed downstairs to get a soda before going to church. I decided to take the elevator since I thought it would be faster. To my surprise, it stopped on the sixth floor, and the doors opened. In walked one of the football players that had gone up and disappeared with the unconscious girl a few weeks earlier. The girl was with him.

I was glad to see that she was still alright, but when we reached the lobby, I explained that visitation was not available until 8 AM on Sundays. I had to write both of them up, which took a while, but it was worth it to know the location of the two football players. I could keep an eye on them.

Afterward, I returned to the room and hurried to prepare for church. It turned out to be another great service!

CHAPTER 9

THE FISHING TRIP

It was Saturday morning, and I was excited about going fishing for the first time in several years. In Arizona, where I grew up, I spent most of my memorable years with my foster parents. I only got to fish a few times with friends because my foster parents never seemed to want to do anything to really bond with me. Now I understand why. They don't even call me anymore since I moved away to college.

To be honest, it left a hole in my heart. I guess it was always there, but now I had God living inside me, and he was beginning to really fill it up! For the first time in my life, I felt truly loved and excited about fishing. I could not get anybody to go with me because everybody wanted to stay at the university that weekend. The finals were only a few short weeks away.

Still, I felt I wasn't going alone because my true Father, God, and I would go fishing together. Also, the dream showed me that I would catch a huge fish, and my dreams hadn't steered me wrong yet. I couldn't wait to bring that big bass back to the dorm and clean it on my front porch so all the guys could see it. It was going to be a great weekend!

I started the day off with a prayer, asking God for protection and for His mercy, especially when it came to my old Pinto. The lake I was going to is 65 miles from the university. It was still very early as I put my new fishing rod and tackle box in the car. I had to slam the trunk three times before I finally got it to shut.

Before I got in, I thanked God again for the car, especially the new tires. At least I did not have to worry about having a flat on the way. I tried to crank the car, but it refused to turn over. After several minutes, I took a break and prayed.

"God," I said, "if you want me to go fishing, let my car start.

I'm going to try it one more time."

Then I turned the key and wham! After a few noises and clucks, it turned over and started. Finally, I was off on my adventure. Along the way, as the sun rose higher and higher, I noticed the sky looked ominously dark and cloudy. The wind was driving hard, and the clouds were heavy and black. I turned on my radio and listened to the local Christian station. They were singing a song about filling up the barrel and letting it rain. This was referring to a spiritual blessing, not literal rain. Either way, it did not sit well with me seeing all the black clouds in the sky!

After driving about fifty miles, I turned off on the back road that led to the lake. The road was curvy, and I had to go slowly since the wind was gusting. I was not sure how I would catch a fish in that weather, but I would have faith and try, since the dream told me to go fishing. I started to wonder if I was becoming a nut for Jesus like Mike and Jeff, but I guessed that it was not a bad thing.

Finally, I found a good parking place by the lake. Of course, there was an old, dilapidated sign that read "No Fishing." I assumed the sign was outdated since this was a popular fishing site. I decided to ignore it and trust my dream. I parked right by the sign to hide it from view and headed down the path toward the lake.

It was about a quarter-mile walk to the lake, and after several minutes, I found a great spot on a wharf that was only a few feet wide. It was timeworn and craggy, but it went out about fifteen feet into the lake from the shore. Some weeds were growing around it, and it looked safe enough to fish.

I continued out to the end of the narrow wharf and had a seat on an upside-down five-gallon bucket that I had brought for just this purpose. The weather still looked threatening. The wind was blowing hard as I put on my headset and listened to Christian praise and worship music. With my new fishing lure on it, I launched my first cast far out into the lake and slowly reeled it in. I did this repeatedly for several hours and got nothing, not even a nibble on the line.

I was still praising the Lord, listening to the music, casting my line, and not getting even a bite. The clouds grew darker, and the wind gusted harder. In the distance, I saw a strange-looking man. He was dressed in black, riding a horse, and galloping along the lake. He was about a half-mile away and headed straight at me.

For some reason, I was scared for the first time in a while. This moment was even scarier than when I had gone skydiving. I couldn't explain why, but I knew the fearsome rider meant to do me harm.

I began to pray as the man in black grew closer, asking God to protect me, but I would stand my ground in Jesus's name!

As he drew ever nearer, I became terrified because he was still coming straight at me! He was close enough that his face became clearer to me, and on it was a look of pure hate. I wondered if this was death coming for me at such a young age.

As the frightening visage drew nearer, now within just a few feet of me, I reacted not with prayer but with reflexes. I fell off my seat, diving into the lake! When I pulled myself back out of the water, it was pouring, with thunder and lightning crashing all around. The man on the horse had disappeared!

I was glad he was gone, but I was done fishing for the day. I'd had enough and headed back up the path, soaking wet and upset that I was half-drowned. If there was one thing I hated more than heights, it was getting soaked by rain and falling into the lake.

I got back in the car, and after several minutes of trying, it finally started. It was now almost noon, and I drove back to the university, soaking wet and cold in my old car. I asked God what I was supposed to learn from all this. To be honest, I was frustrated over the wasted day.

Who was the strange man on the horse, and what could it mean? Had it all been another of my dreams? When I finally calmed down, I thought for a while, and I guessed the man on the horse represented death. I had always heard that death came in pairs. Maybe two people were going to die? Was it going to be Mike and Jeff? They were the only pair I knew.

Finally, I was back at the dorm only to find there had been a massive hailstorm while I was away fishing. After talking to the residents in the dorm, I learned the hailstorm hit only minutes after I left. Had I not gone fishing, I would have been right in the middle of it.

The hail was huge, with remnants left on the pavement about the size of softballs. Every glass window in town appeared to be broken. I looked over the rail on the

11th floor, and I couldn't see a car in the parking lot with a windshield intact, except for my old Ford Pinto. I even noticed Howie's now pink moped was all dented up. I guessed he should have gone fishing with me after all! I thanked God for letting me survive this bizarre day as I went back to my room to clean up and study for finals.

CHAPTER 10

DEATH

I awoke early Monday morning, glad the weekend was over but also scared of the week to come. I was worried that something bad was going to happen during the coming week. I hurried to get dressed and did my rounds on the floors before leaving the dorm to walk to class.   When daylight came, I hurried down to chemistry class, happy to see Howie on the path ahead of me.

He was actually going to class this week. I arrived at class a few minutes late to find most of the students already in their seats and talking among themselves. Ten minutes later, the professor walked into the room, looking like she had been crying. She briefly explained that there would be no class due to a death in her family. Next Friday, she added, she would give one last chemistry test, which would count for half the grade in the class. She dismissed the class and sent all of us on our way to study.

I left the room and stood in the hallway, talking to the other students about the upcoming test. Like everyone else, I was shocked by the news. It seemed death had struck; it was as if the rider on the black horse by the lake was an omen.   Howie approached me as he entered the hallway. He asked if he could come by Thursday night and study with me. I said sure, but I was wondering why he wanted to study with me since my grade was a C and he was an A. I had no idea why he wanted my help. Still baffled by Howie's question, I went to a few other classes and headed to the lunchroom afterward.

I walked into the cafeteria and noticed a new face at the cash register. I went through the line excited because today, they were serving my favorite meatloaf and mashed potatoes with gravy. As I handed the new cashier my card, I asked, "Where is the older lady, Carolyn, today?"

"I'm Samantha," the lady replied, "Carolyn no longer works here."

"Why? Did she quit?"

"I don't know. I heard she just stopped coming to work, but I don't know anything more about it."

I thanked the cashier and sat down with Jeff and Mike, who were at a nearby table. When I sat down, I realized that they, too, were concerned about Carolyn. Apparently, she'd just stopped coming to work and did not call in. Nobody knew what happened to her. Maybe it was just Carolyn's time to move on.

After several minutes of conversation, we reluctantly moved on to the hard task ahead. We all had finals coming up soon since the semester was coming to an end. Mike said he was really worried about his grades because he had low C's in several classes. Jeff did not seem worried at all. He simply believed that God would take care of it. I was more concerned about chemistry than anything else, so I said my goodbyes and hurried back to the dorm to study.

Late that night, I did my rounds at the dorm and then went to bed early. I had pushed the thoughts of the fishing trip out of my mind by then, replacing them with chemistry formulas and memorized facts. All I could think about were the problems that I was facing the rest of the week in preparation for all of the looming exams.

The next day, I woke up late, so I decided to skip my first class. Instead, I headed to the Wigwam, a small coffee shop on campus where all the students hung out. I needed to clear my head and get ready for the day. I found a couple of residents from the dormitory there drinking coffee, so I engaged in small talk with them for a few minutes. After a few minutes, John, a resident from the 3rd floor, joined in and asked me if I'd heard about Sally

Confused, all I could say was, "Sally?"

"Yeah," John continued, "You know…the pretty ginger that plays tennis all the time. She's in the hospital, and it's not looking good." He went on to explain that she'd had a drug overdose during the past weekend and was not doing well.

It was time for me to head to class, so I told them all goodbye and started walking toward the quad, my head spinning with thoughts. I didn't have time to sort it out then, but later, once class was over, I took some time to gather my thoughts under one of the big oak trees. I sat there just wondering if Sally was what my fishing trip had been all about. Was she going to die? I just had managed to forget about that bad fishing experience, and it was back again. I decided that I needed to go and see Sally tomorrow evening after class. That afternoon, I was heading up to my room, and as I got on the elevator, Mike and Jeff were just getting off. I asked where they were heading. "To the library, of course," Mike answered, "I have lots of studying to do."

I then stopped them and told them about Sally. After talking for several minutes, I asked them if they wanted to go to see her at the hospital with me the following evening. They both said that they had too much studying to do but would be praying for her. They were sure God would heal her. I said goodbye, let the elevator close behind me, and made my way up to the dorm room. After praying for Sally, I spent the rest of the day studying and then turned in for the night.

I awoke early that morning with Sally still on my mind. I had a feeling that something wasn't right. I asked God to help her and to please heal her if it was His will to do so. I prayed that if He was going to take her life, to please make sure she had one more chance to receive Jesus as her Savior. I hurried off to class again, but my mind was on Sally all day. Was this why I'd had the strange, frightening experience at my last fishing trip? Was God preparing me for something?

After a day full of classes, I headed to the hospital as fast as I could get there. Traffic was heavy, and it seemed to take forever, but my old car finally made it. I arrived just before 5 pm and hurried up to the entrance, fearing visiting hours would be over soon. I went to the front desk and asked the young girl there if she would tell me what room Sally was in. Of course, she was. She asked me Sally's last name. I then realized that I had no idea what her last name could be. I talked with the receptionist for several minutes, explaining the situation and why I was there. After a brief search through the new patients' registry, she concluded that Sally was in room 402, on the 4th floor.

I raced upstairs to room 402, deciding not to wait for the elevator. I found the door slightly ajar. As I entered the room, I saw a young lady with familiar red hair in the hospital bed. She had many IV medications, with tubes going into both her arms. She was pale and had her eyes closed. "Sally, it's Steve," I whispered. There was no response, so I repeated, "Sally, it's Steve." This time, she opened her eyes and, in a weak voice, said, "Hi, Steve." After several minutes of small talk, I realized she was in trouble and might not make it. "Sally, are you ready to meet God?"

"No, but I am going to meet him soon," she replied weakly. "Would you like to know Jesus as your Savior?"

"Yes," her response was weak but full of emotion. I knew this was her moment, so I led Sally in the Sinner's Prayer.

After we prayed, there was a knock at the door, and two young nurses entered the room. They asked me to leave for a minute while they gave Sally her evening medicine. I excused myself, telling Sally I would be right back, and found a seat in the waiting area by the 4th-floor nursing station. I said hello to the elderly nurse at the station and then passed the time by staring out the window, deep in thought. I was just looking at the trees and thinking about all of the beautiful things God had made. For some reason, they seemed brighter and more colorful than ever before.

After about five minutes, I returned to the room to find the door ajar again. I looked in the room and found the nurses were no longer there. I spoke to Sally as I approached the bed again. She had a strange glow on her face but was not moving at all this time. I began to yell as I shook her, trying to wake her. She was not breathing! I guess I was loud enough because the nurse who was at the station came into the room. She called a code blue and asked me to wait outside. Several doctors and nurses hurried into Sally's room and shut the door. I sat back in the chair by the window and began to pray as I again gazed out at God's creation.

After about 30 minutes, all the doctors and nurses left Sally's room. As they left, they took Sally with them. She was covered by a blanket, motionless on the bed. I watched in shock as they pushed her into the open elevator and took her away. One of the Doctors caught my eye and approached, asking if I was a relative. "No, just a friend," I replied. He walked away, mumbling, "I'm truly sorry about your friend."

Now, everyone but the elderly nurse was gone. She was back at the nurse's station, looking somber. I asked her if I could talk to the two young nurses who had gone into Sally's room a few minutes before she died. With a strange look on her face, she replied, "Young man, I have been the only nurse at this station for the past hour. I don't know what you are talking about."

I responded that I must have been mistaken. I thanked her for her help, and I turned and walked away. As I left the hospital, I was very confused about the two young nurses. I was sure I had seen them, but who were they? Why had they been there? I guessed I would never know.

CHAPTER 11

HOWIE'S SECRET IS DISCOVERED

It was Monday morning, and I slept in because there were no classes that week due to finals starting on Thursday. I will take my Chemistry Final on Thursday morning at 10 am. This was the only test that concerned me because the grade counted twice since the teacher went home early due to a death in the family. However, she will return to give the final test on Thursday. This would be a challenge because if I could ace the final, I might be able to pull my grade up to an A-. Still, I knew there would not be a curve because Howie always made a very high score.

I finally got out of bed, and as I started walking to the shower, I noticed a large, yellow envelope pushed under the door. As I picked it up, I noticed a note on the outside that read, "From Howie. This was my Chemistry study guide. Please try to fill it out, and I will get with you

Tuesday afternoon to study with you". I was excited to study with Howie because he always did extremely well on the exams. I ripped the package open to find just three pages inside. It looked just like a test without the answers filled in. The date on the top of the first page was Thursday's date. It had a space to write your name. Wow! Could this be the test? What was Howie up to? I read the first question, but I started feeling very guilty immediately, so I put it back in the envelope and headed to the shower.

After my shower, I got dressed and headed out for my usual morning walk. I liked to go walking in the morning to pray and clear my head. I found it was a great time to talk to God and just enjoy his creation. On that day, **I could not get the first question out of my mind, which was:**

The Definite shape and volume of particles packed tightly together: Liquids.

_____True

_____*False*

I knew God would not approve of having the test before I took it. I had a big choice to make. Would I use this test or trust God and go on my own? I decided to leave the so-called "study guide" in the envelope until Howie came by tomorrow afternoon. I needed to ask him a few questions about it before I filled it out. I knew if this was a stolen test and I used it, God would not be very proud of me.

Later that day, I went by the cafeteria only to find Jeff and Mike already eating at a table. It was good to see them again. I sat with them, and we began to talk about the day. I started to tell them about the study guide that Howie left me, but I kept quiet. In fact, I didn't have much to add to the conversation at all. Of course, Jeff noticed after only a few minutes, "Steve, you look like you have something on your mind."

"Finals are stressing me out…especially chemistry," was my answer. Jeff and Mike finished eating and left the table. As I finished, I could not get my mind off

of Howie. How did he get the test? Was it really the test or

a joke? Howie had never played jokes on me before, so I

knew it was the real thing.

I had trouble sleeping that night, and I woke up early

the next day. It was very stormy, so I stayed in and studied

Chemistry all morning.   As much as I was tempted, I did

not dare open the package from Howie again. I just knew

that something was not right with it. If I got caught with the

test, I might get expelled from college. I had not been

following God all that long, but I knew having the test

beforehand would not sit well with Him. If I was going to

follow Jesus and have him as my Savior, I had to try to live

my life the way He would want me to!

After studying for many hours, I stopped for lunch.

As I was making a couple of sandwiches in my tiny kitchen,

I heard a knock at the door. I laid down the half-completed

sandwich and went to open the door. Howie was standing

there, but he had no books to study. I invited him inside and offered him one of my sandwiches, which he gladly accepted.

"Did you get a look at the study guide I left under the door?" Howie asked between bites. It was the question I had been dreading, but I needed to face this situation head-on.

"Yes, but I have not filled it out yet," I replied, also between bites. The sandwich suddenly felt like a lump in my throat.

"Why not?" Howie's voice sounded shocked. He put the rest of his sandwich down on the table, staring directly at me.

"Howie, this looks like it's the test. What's up with this?" I had to find out what was going on, but I was not prepared for his response.

"Steve, this is the test." His blunt reply shocked me, but there was even more than I could have guessed.

"I'm graduating soon, and I'll need somebody to take over my business. You see, I got the test from the grad students that assisted the teachers. I'm in every department at the university except pharmacy. I can hook you up with all of my connections and teach you how to sell the tests to the students without getting caught. I only have one semester left, and I think you would be a great choice for taking over the business. Steve, the students need the tests, and, believe me, they pay well for them."

I was speechless. I simply could not believe what I was hearing. I never would have guessed that Howie would be so dishonest. He was basically a crook! Perhaps mistaking my silence for contemplation, he made a final attempt at convincing me to take his place. "Steve, you have really been good to me, and I want to pay you back by giving you my business after I graduate. So, what do you say?" Finally managing to clear the lump in my throat, I handed the envelope back to Howie, "I'm a Christian, and I can't do this!" Howie looked both shocked and angry. He stormed toward the door, slamming it as he left the room.

It was the night before the chemistry test, and I went to sleep early. That night was one to remember. I had a very strange dream. I was in a classroom full of students. My Chemistry teacher was having a review for the final exam. She wrote each question on the board and explained every answer to the class in great detail. It was such a long and thorough dream that I was tired when I awoke. I had to hurry to get to class in time to take the exam. I was the last one there. The teacher was passing out the tests as I sat down.

"You have 90 minutes to take your test," explained Mrs. Jones, "but I wanted to let you know that it has been a good semester, and I thank you all for working with me due to the death in my family. This test shouldn't be all that difficult for you if you studied. I wish you all the best."

She further explained that the grades would be posted on the door after 4 pm that afternoon, using the last four digits of our social security numbers. As I started the test, I could not help but notice the only question I remembered from Howie's test was slightly different, but all the other questions were the same as in my dream. Howie and I were the first to finish and turned in our papers at about the same time.

As I left the room, Howie yelled, "Stop!" I turned back to find an angry Howie hovering over me. He asked me if I had told the teacher about the test, and he'd shown me. I could tell he was trying to control his anger but wasn't being very successful.

"No," I answered simply, but I had noticed the only question I'd seen from the yellow envelope test was slightly changed, making the answer different. Instead of liquids, the teacher had changed the last word to solids.

"Yes, all the questions were changed slightly,"

Howie growled. "I think I failed it, and it's entirely your fault!"

"I didn't tell. If you failed it, that's your business," was my response. Whether he believed me or not, I couldn't say. I started sharing with Howie about Jesus, and he got even angrier, storming away.

Later that day, I returned to find I had made a 100% on the test, with the next best grade being an 82. It was unbelievable. I had beat everyone else's grade on the exam by 18 points or more! I thanked God and hurried back to study for my next test.

CHAPTER 12

THE END OF THE SEMESTER

I awoke early the morning after finals were over. It was a great feeling! My first semester was finished, and I had no more stress or worries for at least a month. After watching all the residents pack up and head out, I decided to go over to the cafeteria for one last meal before it closed for the semester. When I arrived at the cafeteria, it was almost closing time. I hurried through the line, loading everything on my plate like it was the last meal I would eat that year. I looked over at one of the corner tables, and I saw some familiar faces.

Jeff and Mike were having a final meal before heading back home, too. I went over and sat with them. They both said they were grabbing a bite before the long trip back to Monroe, Louisiana. I told them that I would be staying over the break to watch over the dorm and that I would see them when they got back. We all finished lunch and went our separate ways.

Late that afternoon, I decided to take a ride around town just to pass the time. I was driving around campus in my old car when, all of a sudden, the engine just stopped. It was just like I ran out of gas or something, but the tank was half full. I jumped out and pushed my car off the main road. This was definitely not what I needed. I was almost broke, and God only knew how much this would cost me. I walked to the cafeteria and used the payphone on the outside wall to call the garage and have my car towed in for repairs. They told me it would be a few days before they could look at it, but they'd call me with an estimate as soon as they could. It was kind of sad to watch the car leave under tow. I just did not understand why God would allow this to happen so close to the end of the semester. Still, if it had to happen, at least the car broke down while school was not in session.

I decided to take a few days and just relax and wait for the repair shop to call me about the car. I went to the top of my dorm building and sat on the corner, letting my feet hang off the roof. The roof was flat, so there was no chance I would fall. I was so thankful to God for getting me over my fear of heights. If it had not been for Mike and Jeff taking me skydiving, that would have never happened. I knew God sent them to me for that very reason. It was nice to just sit and enjoy the view and think about all God had done for me.

The next morning, around 8 am, my phone rang. It was the repair shop. The voice on the phone was an older man. He said that my car was ready.

"You were supposed to call me with a price first," I replied, a little annoyed.

"How much do I owe you?"

The voice on the other end laughed and said, "Nothing. Just come and pick it up. I will explain everything when you get here." I hung up, hardly believing my ears. My car was fixed, and I owed nothing?

After lunch, I called a cab and rode over to the repair shop. As I was getting out of the cab, I noticed everybody in the garage was looking at me. It was almost like the president had pulled up. As I walked into the customer service office, the manager greeted me and took out a bag from under the counter.

"I found this under your car, pushed into the back wheel well," he explained. "The way it was placed in the small hole under the car, the fuel line was getting smashed, and fuel could not get to the engine properly. I took what you owe us from the money in the bag. I looked into the bag and could hardly believe my eyes! There must be at least $10,000 in there. Did you put the money under the car for safekeeping?"

"No," I answered. I got it at a government auction, and apparently, it was taken from the owner by the FBI during a crime. I guess the criminal hid the money really well from the police." We both had a good laugh as I drove off. When I got back to the dorm, I carried the bag back to my room and counted the money. It was exactly $11,100 dollars. I put 10% aside to give to God in the Sunday offering plate, silently giving Him thanks for everything. After all the good He had done for me, I really could not wait for Sunday to give that 10%!